Beneath the Ashen Sky

A Novella

Philip Mazza

Also by Philip Mazza

From Under a Tree
Book One; The Harrow Saga

Shadow in the Flame
Book Two; The Harrow Saga

Children at the Gate
Book Three; The Harrow Saga

The Child of Fire
Book Four; The Harrow Saga
(Coming 2025)

The Neon Hive

The Quantum Gardener

At the End of it All

Beneath the Ashen Sky

A Novella

Philip Mazza

OMNI PUBLISHERS

Omni Publishers of New York
ISBN 978-0-9977109-3-9
Printed in the United States of America

First Printing: December 2024

For those who have faced the darkness and still hold on to the light of memory. To the brave souls who endured separation yet found strength in love and hope. For my family, whose stories echo in my heart, reminding me that even in despair, compassion can illuminate the path forward. And to all the children who dream of home, may you always carry your memories like stones in your pocket.

From the author

This story has been with me for as long as I can remember, a haunting melody that has played on repeat in the recesses of my mind. It's a tale I never wanted to write, but one I knew I had to tell, a duty I could not shirk.

I first heard about the trains when I was a boy, not much older than Jakob, I suppose. My father spoke of them once. His eyes went distant like he was seeing something far away, something terrible. He didn't say much, but what he did say stayed with me.

For years, I tried to forget. But the trains kept coming back, rumbling through my dreams. I'd hear the screech of metal on metal, smelling the fear and desperation of people packed into cattle cars.

I wrote this story because I had to. Because the voices of those who rode those trains deserved to be heard. Because the world needs to remember, even when the memories have been so far removed by time.

It's not an easy tale. Just people, ordinary people, caught in the machinery of hatred and indifference. A boy torn from his family. An old man offering what comfort he can in the face of unspeakable horror.

I wanted to show the small moments of humanity that can exist even in the darkest places. The strength that can be found in a kind word, a shared story, a hand held in the dark. Because that's what we have, in the end. Our connections to each other. Our ability to choose kindness, even when the world has shown us none.

I don't pretend to understand any of this. To offer answers to the darkness that sometimes rips through man. I can't explain why such evil exists in the world, or how people can turn away from the suffering of others. All I can do is bear witness. To say, "This happened. These people lived. They mattered. We must learn from this."

Writing this story felt like moving through a dark tunnel, mile after mile with no end in sight. There were moments when I thought about stopping, about choosing something simpler. Wizards and swords, hovercars in futuristic cities - those stories come easier, sliding across the page without much trouble. But I kept going, because I owed it to Jakob and Moshe, to all the real people they represent.

I hope that those who read this story will see themselves in Jakob and Moshe. That they'll feel the fear, the desperation, the small moments of connection that can mean the difference between giving up and holding on for one more day.

Most of all, I hope this story makes people think. To think about the choices we make, the kind you live with. The kind you can't outrun or forget. To think about what happens when you turn your back on someone else's pain and act like it's not your problem. I want people to think about what we owe each other, not as strangers, but as people trying to share the same world. To think about what happens when you hand power to people who will twist it in their hands until it breaks.

So, here's the story I leave with you. It won't be an easy journey, but it's one I believe is worth taking. Because in the end, it's not just Jakob's story, or Moshe's. It's our story. It belongs to all of us. A reminder of what we've lost, what we've endured, and what we must never forget.

Separation

The screams came in the night. Jakob woke. His heart beat fast. He thought it was a dream. It wasn't.

"Mama?" he said. The room was dark.

No answer. More screams. Closer now. Boots on the street.

Jakob got up. The floor was cold. He went to the window. He looked out.

Soldiers were in the street. They wore dark uniforms. They broke down doors. They pulled people from houses. Neighbors he knew were being taken.

"Jakob!" His mother came in. Her hair was wild. Her eyes were afraid. "We must go!"

She took his arm. They went to the door. Ana was there. They held each other.

"What's happening?" Ana said.

"Quiet now," their mother said. Her voice shook.

They went down the stairs. Jakob's heart was loud. At the bottom, the front door broke open.

"Out! Fast!" A soldier said. He had a gun.

Their mother pushed them behind her. "Please," she said. "They're children."

The soldier didn't care. He took their mother's arm. He pulled her. Jakob lost her hand.

"Mama!" he said. He reached for her.

People pushed him. He couldn't see his mother. He couldn't see Ana. He was alone.

They went to the train station. People cried. Soldiers shouted. The train was there. He glanced at the sky. It was gray.

It wasn't a normal train. The railcars were like boxes. They had small windows with bars.

"Move!" A soldier pushed Jakob.

He almost fell. He saw he was going to a railcar.

"No!" Jakob said. "I need my mama!"

No one listened. Someone picked him up. They put him in the railcar. He hit the floor hard.

Jakob got up. It was full of people. It was dark. It smelled bad.

He pushed through people. He got to a window. He looked out. He tried to find his family. They weren't there.

The train started to move. Jakob kept looking. He couldn't see them.

"Mama!" he said. No one heard him.

A woman touched his shoulder. "Be quiet," she said. "Save your strength."

Jakob looked at her. He was crying. "My family," he said. "I can't find them."

"I know," she said.

Jakob looked out again. The platform was empty now. His family wasn't there.

The train went faster. Jakob felt sick. He was alone.

He sat down. People around him cried. Some prayed. Some were quiet.

Jakob looked at them. An old man prayed. A mother held a baby. Two boys held each other.

He thought about his family. He remembered his mother's face. Her smile. Her songs. Ana's playful smile and giggle. His father's laugh.

He cried again. He wiped his eyes. He had to be strong.

The train kept going. People were quiet now. It was hard to breathe.

Jakob was hungry. He was tired. He didn't know where they were going.

He fell asleep. He dreamed of home. Of his family.

When he woke up, he was still on the train. It was still dark. People were still quiet.

He felt something in his pocket. It was a stone. His father gave it to him when they were in a park. He held it tight.

Jakob remembered looking at the stone, turning it over in his fingers. "What's it for?"

His father looked at him. "It's to remind you of me," he said. "When you hold it, remember to be strong. Like this stone."

Jakob frowned a little, confused. "Strong?"

"Yes, " his father said. "Life's going to ask a lot of you. More than you'll think you can give. But you be hard when you need to be. Be brave. Don't break "

He held the stone tighter. "I won't."

The train kept going. Jakob didn't know where. He saw trees and hills outside.

People were afraid. They were hungry and thirsty. Children cried quietly.

Jakob thought about his mother. What would she say? Be brave, he thought. Be strong.

A woman smiled at him. "What's your name?" she said.

"Jakob," he said.

"I'm Sarah," she said. "No more tears."

Jakob nodded. He looked around. People were helping each other.

He decided to be brave. Like his father. Like the stone. To be kind. Like his mother. To have hope.

The wheels clacked against the tracks. It was a steady rhythm. Like a heartbeat. Jakob listened to it. He thought about his father's watch. How it ticked. How his father would wind it every night.

The sun came up. Light came through the small windows. It made long shadows on the floor. Jakob could see people's faces now. They looked tired. Scared. But some smiled at him.

An old man with a hat sat next to Jakob. He had white hair. Kind eyes.

"You're a brave boy," the old man said.

Jakob didn't feel brave. But he nodded.

"I had a grandson like you," the old man said. "He was brave too."

"Where is he now?" Jakob asked.

The old man looked sad. He didn't answer.

Jakob understood. He took the old man's hand. It was rough. Warm.

The train stopped sometimes. But they couldn't get out. Soldiers brought water. Not much food. It wasn't enough.

People got sick. The air was bad. It smelled worse now.

Jakob tried to be helpful. He gave his water to a mother with a baby. He helped an old woman stand up. It made him feel better. Stronger.

Time passed. Hours. But how many? Jakob couldn't tell. The train kept going.

Jakob held the stone tight and thought about his father.

The old man taught Jakob a prayer. Jakob didn't know if he believed in God anymore. But he said the prayer anyway. It made him feel closer to home.

Sarah told stories. About her life before. About her family. Jakob listened. He tried to remember every word. Every detail. It was important. He didn't know why. But it was.

The train kept going. Through forests. Past towns. Jakob saw people sometimes. They looked away. Or they stared. He wondered if they knew. If they cared.

He was hungry all the time now. His stomach hurt. But he tried not to complain. Others had it worse.

At night, he dreamed of his mother's cooking. Of Shabbat dinners. Of his father reading to him. He woke up crying sometimes. But quietly. He didn't want to wake the others.

The train kept going. Jakob didn't know where. But he wasn't alone. He had his memories. His stone. The old man's prayer. Sarah's stories. It wasn't much. But it was something. It was hope.

Friend

The train stopped. It was dark inside. Jakob stood pressed against others. The smell was bad. He couldn't breathe well. The air was thick with sweat and fear. It clung to his skin like a damp cloth.

The door opened. A soldier looked in. No water or food this time. The door slammed shut, the iron lock clicking with a sharp, metallic thud. It was loud. Final.

The train started, slowly at first. The wheels made a noise. A rhythm. Like a heartbeat. Steady. Relentless.

Jakob wanted to yell for his mother. He couldn't. His throat was tight. Dry. Words wouldn't come. Just a silent scream in his head.

Someone touched his shoulder. It was the old man with the hat. His eyes were bright. They held something. Wisdom maybe. Or just old pain.

"Be calm, boy," the old man said. His voice was low. Rough. Like gravel. "Fear won't help."

Jakob breathed hard. His chest hurt. "I can't. My family." The words came out broken.

"I know," the old man said. His hand stayed on Jakob's shoulder. Steady. "Be strong. For them."

"Who are you?" Jakob asked. He needed to know. Needed something to hold onto.

"I didn't tell you my name, did I," the old man said. Simple. Direct. "Inconsiderate of me. My name is Moshe. What's your name?"

"Jakob."

"Good name," Moshe said. He nodded. Once. "You'll need strength now."

The train moved again. A jolt.

People cried out. Bodies pressed closer. Jakob felt crushed. Moshe held him close. His body was thin but solid.

"Stay with me," Moshe said. His breath was warm on Jakob's ear. "We'll get through this."

Jakob nodded. He couldn't speak. His throat was too tight.

He stayed close to Moshe. It helped a little. Not much. But a little was all he had.

Time passed. It was hard to tell how much. There was no light now. No day or night. Just the constant motion of the train. The press of bodies. The smell of fear.

Jakob slept sometimes. It wasn't real sleep. Just a kind of darkness. When he was awake, Moshe talked to him. His voice was low. Steady. It gave Jakob something to focus on.

"What do you want to be, Jakob?" Moshe asked. His eyes were on Jakob's face. Watching.

"A doctor. Like my father." The words hurt. They tasted of home. Of things lost.

"Good dream," Moshe said. He nodded. "Keep it. Dreams make us human."

Jakob cried. He couldn't help it. The tears came hot and fast. "How can I dream now?"

Moshe held his hand. His grip was strong. "Your family is in your heart. Remember them."

"What if I forget?" The fear of forgetting was worse than anything.

"You won't," Moshe said. His voice was firm. Certain. "Every night, say their names. Remember their faces."

Jakob nodded. "Yes." He would do it. He had to.

"Good," Moshe said. "Tell me about them."

Jakob talked. He told him about his father. His hands. Strong but gentle. How they looked when he wrote prescriptions. His deep laugh. About his mother. Her smile. The way she sang when she cooked. About his sister. How she always knew when he was sad. As he talked, he could see them. They were there. In the darkness of the train.

When he finished, Moshe squeezed his hand. "See? They're with you."

"Thank you," Jakob said. The words weren't enough. But they were all he had.

The train moved again. Another jolt. People cried out. Jakob felt scared. The fear was always there. Just under the surface.

Moshe held him. His arms were thin but strong. "Breathe, Jakob. This will pass."

Jakob breathed. In and out. Slow. The fear lessened. Not gone. But less.

"I'm hungry," Jakob said. His stomach hurt. Empty.

"We all are," Moshe said. His voice was flat. Matter of fact. He looked at a man with a bag, bread peeking from the top. The man held it close. Guarded.

"Will he share?" Jakob asked. He knew the answer. But he had to ask.

"No," Moshe said. Simple. Direct.

"Why not?"

"Men only share what they don't need," Moshe said. His voice was tired. Old.

The train kept moving. It didn't stop. The rhythm of the wheels was constant. Jakob stayed close to Moshe. It helped. Not much. But enough.

As Jakob fell asleep, Moshe spoke softly. His words were a whisper in the dark. "Rest, Jakob. Remember. If we remember, we're free."

Jakob slept. He dreamed of his family. Of what was lost. Of what might come. But Moshe was there. In the dream. In the dark. It gave him hope. A small flame. But it burned.

The train moved on. They didn't know where. The destination was unknown. Uncertain. But Jakob wasn't alone. For now, that was enough. It had to be.

The darkness pressed in. The air grew thicker. Heavier. But Jakob breathed. In and out. Slow. Steady. Like Moshe taught him. He said the names in his head. Over and over. A prayer. A promise. Father. Mother. Sister. He wouldn't forget. He couldn't. He squeezed the stone in his pocket.

The train rolled on. Into the night. Into the unknown. But Jakob held onto the names. The memories. They were his light in the darkness. His strength in the fear. As long as he had them, he wasn't lost. Not completely.

Shadows

The train moved through the night. Inside, people pressed together. The air was bad. It smelled of fright and dirt.

Jakob sat against the wall. He was small next to the grown-ups. His eyes were dull now. They had lost their shine. Moshe sat next to him. The old man's face was tired but strong.

Moshe leaned close. His voice was low. "Eat, boy. To live is to fight."

Jakob looked at the bread in Moshe's hand. It was hard and moldy. His stomach turned. He was hungry but the bread looked bad.

"I can't," Jakob said. His voice broke. "It's not right."

Moshe's eyes were kind. "Nothing here is right. But we must live. We must go on."

Jakob glanced around the car. The man with the bag lay still, his face pale, blood trickling slowly from his nose. The bag was on the floor, its contents scattered - clothing, small trinkets, things that once mattered.

Jakob looked around. He saw the man with the bag. He was asleep, the bag on the floor, contents spilled.

The train rounded a sharp curve. The metal screamed. People moved. A woman cried out.

"We'll all die! They're taking us to the camps!"

People got scared. Jakob felt cold inside. He looked at Moshe. He had heard his parents talking about the camps, where people went to die.

Moshe spoke loud and clear. "Be quiet. Your fear helps them. We must not let them win."

"He's right," someone said.

It got quiet. People cried softly. The train kept moving. Moshe broke the bread. He gave half to Sarah who was nearby. She took it. She looked thankful and ashamed.

"Tell me a story," Jakob said. "Please. Like before."

Moshe nodded. "I'll tell you about the time I crossed the desert. I had only a camel and the stars."

The old man's eyes twinkled as he told his tale. "On the third night, I encountered a Bedouin family . . ."

"What is Bedouin?" Jakob interrupted.

"They are a people who live in the desert. They roam from one place to another."

"They don't have a home?"

Moshe smiled, eyes wide. "The whole desert is their home. So, when I met them, they were stranded with a broken water skin. Without hesitation, I shared my meager water supply. Their gratitude was immeasurable."

Moshe paused. "As we parted ways, the father pressed a small pouch into my hand. 'For your kindness,' he said. Inside was a map leading to an oasis, hidden from most travelers."

"That oasis sustained me for the remainder of my journey. But more importantly, it taught me that even in the harshest conditions, a single act of compassion can ripple outward, touching lives in ways we may never fully comprehend."

Jakob felt less scared. He closed his eyes. Moshe's voice made things better for a while.

The train rolled on. Its wheels clicked against the tracks. The sound was steady. It was like a heartbeat. A heartbeat of iron and steel.

Jakob tried to picture the desert. The sand. The stars. It was hard. All he could see was the inside of the train car. The dirty faces. The scared eyes.

"Tell me about the desert."

Moshe's voice was low. It was steady. It was like a rope in the dark. Jakob held onto it.

"The desert is big," Moshe said. "Bigger than you can imagine. At night, the stars come out. They fill the sky. You feel small. But you also feel part of something big."

Jakob tried to imagine it. The big sky. The stars. It was hard. The railcar was small. The air was thick. It was hard to breathe.

"How do you find your way?" Jakob asked.

Moshe smiled. It was a small smile. But it was real. "You learn to read the stars. They're like a map in the sky. If you know how to look, they'll always show you the way."

Jakob nodded. He didn't understand. Not really. But he wanted to. He wanted to believe there was a way. A way through this darkness.

The train kept moving. It never stopped. Day turned to night. Night turned to day. It was all the same inside the railcar.

People got sick. The smell got worse. Jakob tried not to breathe too deep. He tried not to think about it.

Moshe kept talking. He told stories. About the desert. About the sea. About cities Jakob had never seen. Places he might never see.

"Why do you tell these stories?" Jakob asked.

Moshe looked at him. His eyes were serious. "Because stories are important. They keep us human. They remind us there's more to the world than this."

Jakob thought about that. He thought about the world outside the train. It seemed far away. Like a dream.

The train rolled on. The wheels clicked. Click-clack. Click-clack. It never stopped.

Jakob slept. He dreamed of home. Of his mother's smile. His father's laugh. He woke up crying.

Moshe was there. His hand on Jakob's shoulder. "It's okay," he said. "It's okay to cry."

Jakob wiped his eyes. He felt ashamed. "I'm not a baby," he said.

Moshe nodded. "No, you're not. You're brave. Braver than you know."

The train kept moving. Always moving. Never stopping.

People talked in whispers. They wondered where they were going. What would happen when they got there.

Jakob tried not to listen. He tried to remember Moshe's stories. The desert. The stars. The big sky.

The train rolled on. Into the night. Into the unknown.

Primal

The train rumbled on. Its wheels clacked against the rails. The sound never stopped. Inside the railcar, the air was thick. It smelled of sweat and piss and tragedy. People were packed tight. There was no room to move.

Jakob sat with his back against the wall. Moshe was next to him. The old man's breathing was labored. Jakob could feel the heat from Moshe's body. It was too hot in the car.

"I'm still hungry," Jakob said. His voice was low. He didn't want the others to hear.

Moshe nodded. He reached into his pocket. His hand came out with a small piece of bread. It was hard and stale. Moshe broke it in half. He gave the bigger piece to Jakob.

"Eat," Moshe said.

Jakob looked at it. He was hungry. But he thought that Moshe needed it more. He was old.

"You eat it," Jakob said.

Moshe shook his head. "No. You're young. Still growing."

Jakob ate the bread. It was gone too fast. His stomach still felt empty.

A man stood up. He wore a long coat and was thin. His eyes were wild. He looked around the car. His gaze settled on another man. This man was holding something.

"Give it to me," the thin man said. His voice was rough.

The other man clutched something to his chest. "No," he said. "It's all I have left."

The thin man lunged. They fell to the floor. People around them moved back. There wasn't much room to move.

The fight was over quickly. The thin man stood up. He had a small package in his hand. The other man lay on the floor. He was crying, blood dripping from his nose.

"Why do men fight?" Jakob asked.

Moshe didn't answer right away. He squinted, his face lined and still. Then he shifted a bit on the wood.

"They fight for all sorts of reasons," he said. "Some fight because they have to. Some fight because they want to. Some don't know why."

"But why would they want to?" Jakob asked.

Moshe shrugged. "Pride, sometimes. Or fear. Sometimes they think it's the only way to get what they want."

Jakob thought about that. "Did you ever fight?"

Moshe nodded slowly. "Yes."

"Why?"

Moshe looked at him. "Because I had to."

Jakob frowned. "Were you scared?"

Moshe smiled a little. "Always." He paused. "But you do it anyway."

Jakob kicked his feet out. "Do they always have to fight?"

Moshe shook his head. "No. But sometimes, they don't see any other way."

Jakob was quiet for a long time. "Do you think I'll have to fight?"

Moshe sighed. "I hope not. But if you do, make sure you know why."

Jakob pressed closer to Moshe. Moshe put his arm around Jakob's shoulders.

Night came. The railcar was dark and cold. Jakob couldn't sleep. The train kept moving. It never stopped.

"Moshe," Jakob said. "Where are they taking us?"

Moshe was quiet for a long time. "I don't know," he said finally.

"That woman said something about the camps," Jakob said. "I heard my father and mother talk about the camps once. It's where people go to die."

"Hush now," Moshe told him. "Get some rest."

More time passed. Maybe days. Maybe a week. Jakob wasn't sure. Time didn't mean much anymore. The train stopped a few more times. Guards gave them water sometimes. Still, never enough.

A woman started screaming. Jakob woke up. The woman was holding something. It was small. It didn't move.

"My baby," the woman cried. "Someone help my baby."

Moshe got up. He walked to the woman. He put his hand on her shoulder. He said something to her. Jakob couldn't hear what it was. He watched as Moshe tried to take the baby from her, but she shook her head, wild with grief.

Jakob shut his eyes. He knew.

When Moshe came back, Jakob asked, "Why is this happening?"

Moshe looked tired. He looked old. "There's evil in the world," he said. "But there's good too. We have to remember that."

The train kept moving. People talked less. They were too tired. Too hungry.

A man by the door shouted. "Look," he said. "I see buildings."

Everyone tried to look. They pushed and shoved. But the train didn't stop. It kept going.

Jakob looked at Moshe. "Will God hear us?" he asked.

Moshe closed his eyes. A tear ran down his face. "He hears," Moshe said. "But I don't know if He'll answer."

Night came again. Jakob knew it was night because it was cold. He moved closer to Moshe.

"Tell me a story," Jakob said.

Moshe's voice filled the car, weaving a tale of struggle and resilience:

"In ancient times, there was a humble shepherd named Amos. Though poor, he had a keen sense of justice. One day, he witnessed the king's men oppressing a widow. Without hesitation, Amos spoke up, risking his life to defend her.

His courage inspired others. Soon, a movement grew, with people from all walks of life standing up for the downtrodden. The king, moved by their unity, had a change of heart. He implemented reforms, ensuring fair treatment for all.

Years later, during a great famine, it was the former king who found himself destitute. To his surprise, the same widow Amos had once defended offered him shelter and food, saying, 'We are all one people.'

Amos's small act of bravery had set in motion a chain of kindness that transformed the entire kingdom."

As Moshe finished, a thoughtful silence filled the car. Jakob nodded, understanding the lesson. Then, Sarah started singing. It was an old song. A lullaby. Her voice was weak. Other people joined in.

Jakob felt tears in his eyes. But for the first time in a long time, he didn't feel only sadness. He felt something else. Something like hope.

The song ended. People were quiet. Some of them slept.

"Sleep now," Moshe said to Jakob. "Tomorrow will be hard too."

Jakob closed his eyes. He thought about the song and Moshe's story. He reached into his pocket and felt the cold stone his father had given him. He thought about hope.

The train kept moving. It didn't stop. But for a little while, the people in the railcar felt like people again. Not just cargo. They remembered they were human.

Jakob didn't know where they were going. He didn't know what would happen. But he knew he wasn't alone. He had Moshe. He had the memory of the song.

The train rolled on through the night. Its wheels kept clacking against the rails. The sound never stopped. But inside the car, something had changed. It was small. But it was there.

Hope. Small and fragile. But alive.

Broken

The train rattled onward, its metal wheels grinding against the tracks in a ceaseless rhythm. Inside the cramped railcar, bodies pressed against one another, the air heavy with the stench of sweat and death. Three people had died. Old people. Some of the men had dragged the bodies to one corner of the car.

Jakob huddled against the wall, his small frame shaking with each jolt of the train. He watched as Moshe cupped a handful of rainwater that had pooled in the railcar. The water was thick with filth, but he drank it regardless. He removed a flask from his coat and steadied his hand as he dipped the flask into the rainwater, watching it fill slowly.

His weathered face, etched with lines of worry, leaned close. "Jakob, my boy, you must drink some water."

"I can't," Jakob whispered, his eyes fixed on a lifeless form across from them. "The smell . . ."

"I know, I know," Moshe soothed, gently tilting the flask to Jakob's lips. "But we must stay strong. We must survive."

The train lurched, sending a ripple of groans through the passengers. Sarah slumped forward, her breath rattling in her chest.

"Is she . . .?" Jakob began, his voice trailing off.

Moshe shook his head. "Not yet, but soon. May God have mercy on her soul."

Jakob stood on wobbly legs. He went to her and kissed her cheek. He thought he saw her smile. He wasn't sure.

Hours passed, marked only by the endless clacking of wheels and the gradual dimming of light through the slats. Jakob drifted in and out of consciousness, his dreams filled with the faces of those who had already succumbed.

He awoke with a start as a woman's anguished cry pierced the air. "She's gone!" The woman stood, trembling, over Sarah, who sat hunched over.

Moshe placed a steadying hand on Jakob's shoulder. "Close your eyes, child. There's nothing we can do."

"But shouldn't we help?" Jakob asked, his voice small and uncertain.

"The only help we can offer now is prayer," Moshe replied, his tone heavy with resignation.

A man stood and dragged her body by the ankles to the corner of the railcar with the other dead.

Later the train stopped. A small amount of water was provided. Moshe filled his flask, keeping his share safely in his coat.

Cold again came – night. The railcar grew quieter, save for the occasional sob or whispered prayer. Jakob curled tighter into himself, trying to block out the world around him.

"Moshe," he murmured, "will we die here too?"

Moshe was silent for a long moment before answering. "I don't know. But as long as we draw breath, we must hold onto hope."

"What hope?" Jakob asked bitterly. "Hope? I don't see hope here. I only see death."

Moshe sighed, his eyes glistening in the dim light. "Hope is not something we see, my boy. It's something we carry within us, even in the darkest of times."

The train continued its relentless journey, bearing its cargo of the living and the dead. Jakob shut his eyes. He held to Moshe's words. He remembered his family's faces. Their names. They were his lifeline in the storm.

As dawn broke, casting weak rays through the cracks, Jakob stirred. The air seemed heavier, the silence more oppressive.

"Moshe?" he called softly, reaching out in the gloom.

The old man's hand found his, squeezing gently. "I'm here, Jakob. I'm still here."

"I had a dream," Jakob whispered. "I saw my mother. She was smiling."

Moshe's voice was thick with emotion. "Hold onto that image, my boy. Let it give you strength."

A keening wail cut through the air, startling them both. "My baby! My precious child!" It was the woman still cradling her dead baby.

Jakob instinctively moved closer to Moshe, burying his face in the old man's coat. "Make it stop," he pleaded. "Please, make it stop."

"Shh, shh," Moshe soothed, stroking the Jakob's matted hair. "Focus on my voice. Remember the stories of our people's strength?"

Jakob nodded weakly. "The Exodus from Egypt."

"Yes, good. Even in slavery, our ancestors held onto hope. And what happened?"

"They were freed," Jakob mumbled.

"That's right. We must be like them now. Strong. Resilient."

The train lurched again, eliciting groans from the weakened passengers. Jakob clung tighter to Moshe, his small body trembling.

"I'm scared," he admitted in a barely audible whisper.

Moshe's arms tightened around him. "It's okay to be scared, Jakob. But remember, fear doesn't make you weak. It's how you face that fear that matters."

As the day wore on, the railcar grew quieter. Those who still lived conserved their energy, speaking only in hushed tones. Jakob drifted in and out of consciousness, lulled by the rhythmic motion of the train.

In his more lucid moments, he caught snippets of conversation around him.

"How long have we been traveling?" someone asked.

"Days? Weeks? I've lost track," came a response.

"Where are they taking us?" another asked.

"Does it matter? Wherever it is, it can't be worse than this," a shout echoed.

Jakob tugged at Moshe's sleeve. "Is that true? Could it be worse?"

The old man's face was grave. "We must prepare ourselves for anything, Jakob. But we must also never lose sight of who we are."

"And who are we?" Jakob asked, his voice small and uncertain.

Moshe's eyes gleamed with a fierce pride. "We are the children of Abraham, Isaac, and Jacob. We are a people who have endured for thousands of years. We are survivors."

As night fell once more, the railcar grew eerily still. Jakob could hear the labored breathing of those around him, punctuated by occasional whimpers of pain or despair.

"Moshe," he whispered, "tell me a story. Please. Like you always do."

The old man cleared his throat. "Very well. Once, long ago, there was a young shepherd named David . . ."

Jakob let the familiar words wash over him, clinging to them like a lifeline. For a moment, he could almost forget the horror that surrounded them.

But reality intruded harshly as a man nearby let out a final, rattling breath. Jakob stiffened, his eyes wide with fear.

"Don't look," Moshe murmured, turning the boy's face away. "Remember the story. Focus on my voice."

Jakob nodded, squeezing his eyes shut. "And David faced the giant Goliath . . ."

"That's right," Moshe encouraged. "David was small, but he was brave. He had faith."

Moshe continued his story through the moans and quiet screams. Two more were dragged to the corner.

As dawn broke once more, Jakob awoke to find the railcar unnaturally still. The constant motion of the train remained, but the human sounds – the breathing, the whispers, the groans – had diminished.

"Moshe?" he called out, his voice cracking.

The old man's response was weak. "I'm here, Jakob. I'm still here."

Jakob struggled to sit up, his limbs stiff and aching. He looked around the railcar, his young eyes taking in the grim scene in the corner.

"There are so many. . ." he trailed off, unable to say the word.

Moshe nodded solemnly. "Yes. May their memories be a blessing."

A woman nearby stirred, her face gaunt and eyes hollow. "Water," she croaked. "Please, water."

Jakob tugged at Moshe.

"We must conserve what little we have left," Moshe said softly.

The boy's face crumpled. "But she's suffering."

Moshe's eyes were filled with sorrow. "We're all suffering, Jakob. We must do what we can to survive."

As the day wore on, the stench in the railcar grew unbearable. Jakob buried his face in Moshe's coat, trying to block it out.

"How much longer?" he mumbled.

Moshe stroked his hair. "I don't know, my boy. But we must endure. We must live to tell our story."

Jakob looked up at him, his eyes filled with a wisdom beyond his years. "Will anyone want to hear it?"

"They must," Moshe said firmly. "The world must know what has happened here. We carry the memories of those who didn't survive. It's our duty to bear witness."

The train continued its relentless journey, carrying its cargo of the living and the dead. Jakob clung to Moshe, drawing strength from the old man's unwavering spirit.

As the night's cold embraced the railcar once more, Jakob whispered, "Moshe, I'm afraid to sleep. What if I don't wake up?"

Moshe's voice was gentle but firm. "You will wake up, Jakob. You will. Our people need you to survive, to remember, to tell our story."

Jakob nodded, his small face set with determination. "I will, Moshe. I promise."

The old man smiled faintly. "Good boy. Now, let me tell you another story. This one is about a man named Moses, who led our people to freedom . . ."

As Moshe's words washed over him, Jakob clung to his father's stone in his pocket. The train rattled on through the darkness, bearing its precious cargo of survivors, storytellers, and witnesses to history.

Echoes

The train rolled on. It had been rolling for what seemed like forever. The wheels clacked against the tracks. The sound never stopped. It was always there. In the dark. In the light. In the cold. In the warmth. When they slept. When they were awake. Always the clacking. Always the rolling.

Jakob lay on the hard wooden floor of the railcar. His body ached. He was hungry. He was thirsty. But mostly, he was tired. So tired. He closed his eyes.

He dreamed.

In his dream, he was home. The kitchen was warm. It smelled like fresh bread. His mother stood at the stove. She was humming. It was a tune he knew. A lullaby she used to sing to him when he was small.

"Mama," he said.

She turned. She smiled. Her smile was like the sun coming out after a storm.

"Jakob," she said. "My sweet boy."

He ran to her. He buried his face in her apron. It smelled like home. Like safety.

"I missed you," he said.

"I know," she said. "I missed you too."

He looked up at her. Her face was blurry. He couldn't see it clearly.

"Mama," he said. "I can't see your face."

"It's alright," she said. "I'm here."

But she wasn't. She was fading. The kitchen was fading. Everything was fading.

Jakob woke with a start. The railcar was dark. Bodies pressed against him. The air was thick and stale. The clacking of the wheels was loud in his ears.

He felt tears on his cheeks. He wiped them away.

"Bad dream?" Moshe's voice was low beside him.

Jakob nodded. Then he thought, Moshe couldn't see him in the dark.

"Yes," he said.

"Do you want to talk about it?" Moshe asked.

Jakob was quiet for a moment. The train rolled on.

"I dreamed about my mother," he said finally.

"Ah," Moshe said. "That's not a bad dream. That's a good memory."

"But it hurts," Jakob said.

"Yes," Moshe said. "Good memories can hurt. But they're important. They remind us of who we are. Where we came from."

Jakob thought about this. The train rolled on.

"Tell me about your mother," Moshe said.

Jakob closed his eyes. He saw her face. This time it was clear.

"She's beautiful," he said. "She has dark hair. And green eyes. When she smiles, her whole face lights up."

"She sounds lovely," Moshe said.

"She is . . ." Jakob said. ". . . was . . . I don't know if . . ."

He couldn't finish. The words stuck in his throat.

"Tell me more," Moshe said. "What else do you remember?"

Jakob took a deep breath. The air was heavy in his lungs.

"She has the most beautiful garden," he said. "So many flowers. Different colors. And she makes the best challah. Every Friday. The whole house smells like bread. On Shabbat, she lights the candles. Her hands are so steady. The flames never flicker."

He paused. The memory was so clear. So real. For a moment, he could almost smell the bread. Feel the warmth of the candles.

"What about your father?" Moshe asked.

Jakob smiled in the dark.

"He's tall," he said. "Taller than anyone I know. He has a big laugh. When he laughs, you can feel it in your chest."

"He sounds like a good man," Moshe said.

"He is," Jakob said. "He taught me how to tie my shoes. How to ride a bicycle. How to throw a ball." He rubbed the stone in his pocket. "How to be brave."

The last word caught in his throat. Brave. He didn't feel brave now.

"You are brave," Moshe said as if he could read Jakob's thoughts. "Remembering takes courage. Never forget who you are. Where you come from. They can't take that from you."

The train rolled on. The wheels clacked and clacked and clacked. The sound filled the silence.

"What about you?" Jakob asked. "What about your family?"

Moshe was quiet for so long that Jakob thought he might have fallen asleep.

"A wife. Two sons. Grandchildren," Moshe said finally. His voice was soft. Sad.

"What were they like?" Jakob asked.

Moshe sighed. It was a heavy sound.

"My wife, Miriam," he said. "She was like a summer day. Warm. Bright. Full of life. She could make flowers grow in the desert."

Jakob tried to imagine this woman. This Miriam who could make flowers grow in the desert. He pictured her standing in a garden, the sun high overhead. Her hands reaching down to the earth, her face glowing like the sun itself. Flowers blooming at her feet where there had been nothing but dust and rock before. He wondered what it would be like to know someone like that.

"And your sons?" he asked.

"David and Eli," Moshe said. "David was the quiet one, always with a book, always thinking. You'd find him in a corner, lost in the words. Eli, though - Eli was wild. He couldn't sit still. Always running, always shouting, always laughing, like the world was something to chase. They both have families."

Jakob paused, watching Moshe's eyes, knowing what came next. "Where are they now?" Jakob asked, even though he already knew.

"Like your family," Moshe said. "Taken away." The words were heavy. Final.

The train rolled on.

"I'm sorry," Jakob said.

"Don't be," Moshe said. "They live in my memories. As long as I remember them, they're not gone. Like I told you."

Jakob thought about this. He thought about his mother's smile. His father's laugh. His little sister's grin.

"Tell me about your sister," Moshe said.

Jakob smiled in the dark.

"Ana," he said. "She's six. She follows me everywhere. Sometimes it's annoying. But mostly it's nice. She thinks I know everything."

"Little sisters are like that," Moshe said. There was a smile in his voice.

"She has curly hair," Jakob said. "And freckles. And when she laughs, she snorts like a pig."

He laughed. The sound was strange in the dark railcar. But it felt good.

"That's good," Moshe said. "Laughter is important. Even here. Especially here."

The train rolled on. The wheels clacked against the tracks. The sound never stopped.

"Moshe," Jakob said. "I know I've asked this before . . ."

But Jakob didn't finish his thought. A tear rolled down his cheek.

Moshe was quiet for a long time.

"I know what you were going to ask," he said finally. "All I know is this. We are more than what happens to us. We are our memories. Our stories. Our love."

Jakob thought about this. He thought about his mother's hands kneading bread. His father's strong arms lifting him onto his shoulders. His sister's small fingers holding his hand. He reached into his pocket and squeezed the stone.

"Tell me more," he said. "Tell me about the world before the war."

So Moshe told him. He told him about bustling markets filled with the scent of spices and the sound of haggling. About quiet synagogues where the air was thick with prayer and history. About streets where children played and old men argued and life went on, day after day.

As Moshe spoke, Jakob could see it all. The world before. The world that was gone now. But not forgotten.

The train rolled on. The wheels hitting against the tracks. Clack . . . clack . . . clack. But for a while, Jakob didn't hear it. He was lost in Moshe's words. In the memories of a world he had never known.

"It sounds beautiful," Jakob said when Moshe finally fell silent.

"It was," Moshe said. "It is. In here." He tapped his head. "And in here." He tapped his chest.

Jakob understood. He closed his eyes. He saw his mother's face. His father's smile. His sister's freckles. He held onto the images. Tight.

The train rolled on. The wheels clacked against the tracks. The sound never stopped.

But in the darkness of the railcar, surrounded by fear and despair, Jakob found something. Not hope, this time. That had faded. But something close to it. Something that felt like strength.

He had his memories. He had Moshe's stories. He had the world before, preserved in words and images. He had the stone his father had given him.

It wasn't much. But it was something. Something they couldn't take away.

The train rolled on. Towards what, Jakob didn't know. But he knew this. He would remember. He would hold onto the memories. The stories. The love.

No matter what came next.

Dark

The train rolled on. A day or two passed. Maybe. Time no longer existed in the cramped, dark railcar. Jakob sat with his back against the rough wooden wall, his legs drawn up to his chest. Moshe was beside him, a solid presence in the chaos.

"Are you hungry?" Moshe asked.

Jakob shook his head. He wasn't hungry. He wasn't anything anymore. Just tired. So very tired.

"You should eat something," Moshe said. He reached into his coat and pulled out a small piece of bread. It was the last. Hard and stale. "Here. Take it."

Jakob took the bread. He held it in his hands, feeling its weight. He didn't eat it. He couldn't eat it. Not with the sounds of suffering all around him.

A woman was crying. She had been crying for days. Her child was dead, but she held it close. It was cold, but she didn't care. Others had tried to take it from her. She wouldn't let them.

"Make her stop," a man said. His voice was hoarse. Angry. "For God's sake, make her stop."

"Leave her be," Moshe told the man. His voice was quiet but firm. "She has lost everything."

The man fell silent. The woman's cries continued.

Jakob looked at the morsel of bread in his hands. He broke it in half as best he could and offered a piece to Moshe.

"No," Moshe said. "I gave that to you."

"Please," Jakob said. "It's the last piece."

Moshe took the bread. He nodded his thanks.

They ate in silence. The bread was tasteless, but it was something. It was life.

The train lurched. Bodies shifted. Someone retched in the corner.

Jakob thought of asking Moshe again where they were going. But he didn't. He knew.

"Will we be okay?" Jakob asked. He knew the answer, but he asked anyway.

Moshe was quiet for a long moment. When he spoke, his voice was heavy. "Of course."

It was a lie. They both knew it was a lie. But it was a kind lie. A necessary lie.

The woman's cries had quieted to soft whimpers. The silence that followed was almost worse.

"Tell me another story," Jakob said. He needed to hear something other than the sound of despair.

Moshe nodded. He cleared his throat. "Once, there was a boy who lived in a small village . . ."

The boy had grown up in poverty, with little education or guidance. Despite his circumstances, he had a kind heart and always tried to help others in need. One day, while walking through the village, he came across an elderly woman struggling to carry her groceries. Without hesitation, he offered to help her.

As they walked together, the woman shared stories of her life and the challenges she had faced. The boy listened intently, realizing that everyone has their own struggles, regardless of age or background. When they reached her home, the woman thanked him and offered him a small coin as payment.

The boy politely declined, saying that helping others was its own reward. Touched by his selflessness, the woman smiled and told him that true wealth comes from compassion and generosity, not material possessions.

From that day forward, the boy continued to seek out opportunities to help others in his village. His actions inspired those around him, creating a ripple effect of kindness throughout the community. Though he had little in terms of worldly goods, the boy discovered that he was rich in spirit and the connections he had forged with his neighbors."

Moshe concluded, "You see, we learn that even in the most humble circumstances, we can find purpose and fulfillment through acts of kindness and compassion towards others."

Jakob shut his eyes. Moshe's words were all he had in the dark.

The train rolled on.

Times passed. Hours or maybe it was minutes. Time had no meaning in the railcar.

A commotion at the far end of the car. Voices raised in anger and fear.

"What's happening?" Jakob asked.

Moshe shook his head. "Stay here," he said. He stood, his joints creaking with the effort.

Jakob watched as Moshe made his way through the crowded car. He couldn't see what was happening, but he could hear the voices.

"She's dead," someone said. "The old woman is dead."

A wail of grief. Another voice added to the chorus of sorrow.

Moshe's voice, calm and steady. "We must move her. Give her some dignity."

Murmurs of agreement. The sound of bodies shifting.

Jakob closed his eyes and covered his ears. He didn't want to see. Didn't want to hear. Didn't want to know.

He felt a jostle by him. He opened his eyes. Moshe was back. The old man's face was drawn, his eyes heavy with sorrow.

"Another one?" Jakob asked.

Moshe nodded. "Yes," he whispered.

Jakob felt something break inside him. It wasn't the first death. It wouldn't be the last. But each one chipped away at his hope.

"Why?" he asked. The question was barely a whisper.

Moshe put his arm around Jakob's shoulders. "There is no why, boy. Not here. Not now."

The train rolled on.

Night fell. Or maybe it was already night. It was hard to tell in the darkness of the railcar. But it was cold. So, it had to be night.

Jakob drifted in and out of sleep. His dreams were filled with faces. His mother. His father. His little sister. Where were they? Were they on another train? Were they already. . .?

He woke with a start. Moshe's hand was on his shoulder.

"Easy, boy," Moshe said. "It was just a dream."

But it wasn't just a dream. It was reality. A nightmare they couldn't wake up from.

"I want to go home," Jakob said. His voice cracked.

Moshe's grip on his shoulder tightened. "I know. I know."

The woman was still holding her dead baby. She sang to it, a lullaby soft and haunting. The sound cut through the air, a raw ache that twisted in Jakob's gut.

"Will we die?" Jakob asked. He needed to know. He needed the truth.

Moshe was quiet for a long time. When he spoke, his voice was barely audible. "I don't know, Jakob. But if we do, we will face the unknown with strength."

Jakob nodded. It wasn't comfort, but it was something. A promise. A connection in the darkness. He squeezed the stone in his pocket.

The train rolled on.

Morning came. Or at least, they thought it was morning. A faint light seeped through the cracks in the car.

The air was reeked with the stench of unwashed bodies and despair. People stirred, waking from a restless sleep.

"Water," someone croaked. "Please, water."

There was no water. There hadn't been water for some time.

Jakob's throat was parched. His lips were cracked and bleeding. But he didn't complain. He saw the others, saw their suffering, and knew his thirst was nothing compared to theirs.

Moshe reached into his coat. He pulled out the flask and kept it close, hidden from the others.

"Here," he said, offering it to Jakob. "Not much left, but it's something."

Jakob took the flask with trembling hands. He raised it to his lips and sipped. It was rainwater, warm and gritty, collected by Moshe over time. But to Jakob, it was the sweetest thing he had ever tasted.

He gave the flask back to Moshe who placed it in his coat. The train rolled on.

Hours passed. The railcar grew hotter as the sun climbed higher. Sweat mingled with tears on dirty faces.

A man started shouting. His words were incoherent, a stream of fear and anger.

"Quiet," someone hissed.

But the man wouldn't stop. He pounded on the walls of the car, screaming for release.

Moshe stood. He made his way to the man, speaking softly. Jakob couldn't hear the words, but he saw the man's shoulders slump. The shouting stopped.

When Moshe returned, his face was grim.

"What did you tell him?" Jakob asked.

Moshe shook his head. "Nothing he didn't already know. Sometimes, people just need to be heard."

Jakob nodded. He understood. In this place of silence and suffering, being heard was everything.

The train rolled on.

Afternoon faded into evening. The heat of the day gave way to the chill of night.

Jakob huddled closer to Moshe, seeking warmth and comfort.

"Do you think they're looking for me?" Jakob asked. He didn't need to specify who "they" were.

Moshe was quiet for a moment. "Yes," he said finally. "I'm sure they are."

It was another lie. A kind lie. But Jakob clung to it like a lifeline.

There was silence between them. But it was a different kind of silence. Not the heavy silence of despair, but a silence filled with shared sorrow.

Jakob felt Moshe's arm tighten around his shoulders.

The train rolled on.

Night deepened. It got colder. The railcar was filled with the sounds of agitated sleep and muffled sobs.

Jakob couldn't sleep. He stared into the darkness, his mind racing.

"Moshe," he whispered. "Are you awake?"

"Yes, Jakob. I'm here."

"I'm scared."

Moshe's hand found Jakob's in the darkness. "I know . . . I know." Moshe was quiet for a long moment. When he spoke, his voice was heavy with truth. "I wish I could tell you that everything will be alright. But I don't know. I can't."

Jakob nodded. He appreciated the honesty, even if it hurt.

"But I can tell you this," Moshe continued. "Whatever happens, we have this time together."

Jakob squeezed Moshe's hand. "Thank you," he whispered.

They sat in silence, hand in hand, as the night wore on.

The train rolled on.

Dawn broke. Another day. Another eternity in this rolling prison.

People stirred, waking again to the dark reality of their situation.

The woman, the one holding her dead child, hadn't moved. She was slumped against a wall, still. Too still.

"I think she's . . ." someone said.

Moshe went to check. He returned with a grim nod.

More tears. More grief. The railcar was heavy with it.

The men came. They were quiet. One took her arms. Another took her legs. They carried her to the corner. The pile was there. It smelled. They put her down gently. A man, older than the others, stepped forward. He held her dead child. Carefully, he placed it in her arms.

The men stepped back. They looked at each other. Stood there for a moment. No one spoke. A silent prayer.

Jakob felt numb. He should feel something, he knew. But he couldn't. There was nothing left inside him.

"Jakob," Moshe said. His voice was urgent. "Look at me."

Jakob raised his eyes to meet Moshe's gaze.

"You must not give up," Moshe said. "No matter what happens, you must not give up. Do you understand?"

Jakob nodded. He heard the words but they felt strangely hollow.

"Say it," Moshe insisted. "Say you won't give up."

"I won't give up," Jakob said. The words tasted like ash in his mouth.

Moshe's eyes softened. "I know it's hard. But we must hold on to hope. Even if we feel it's beyond our reach."

Hope. Jakob had forgotten what that felt like.

The train rolled on.

Midday. The heat was unbearable. People were growing delirious with thirst and hunger.

A sound. Different from the constant rumble of the train. A whistle.

"We're slowing down," someone said. "We're stopping!"

Excitement rippled through the car, bright and painful.

But the train didn't stop. It kept moving, slower now, but still moving.

The hope died as quickly as it had come. The despair that followed was even deeper than before.

Jakob felt something wet on his cheek. He touched it, surprised. He was crying. It had been a day, maybe, since he had cried.

Moshe's arm was around him, holding him close.

"It's okay," Moshe murmured. "Let it out."

So Jakob cried. He cried for his lost family, for the dead in the car. He cried for all of them, trapped in this nightmare with no end in sight. He squeezed the stone in his pocket.

And as he cried, he felt something stir inside him. He felt alive. He didn't know what lay ahead. He didn't know if they would survive. But he knew he wasn't alone. And for now, that was enough.

The train rolled on.

Light

Jakob sat with his back against the rough wood. His legs were numb. His stomach was a hollow ache. Moshe's arm was around his shoulders, but the old man's strength was fading. They all were fading.

A woman coughed. The sound was wet and deep. Nobody spoke. They had run out of words days ago.

Jakob closed his eyes. He tried to remember his mother's face. It was getting harder. The memories were slipping away like water through cupped hands.

"Moshe," he whispered.

"Yes, Jakob?"

"I'm hungry."

Moshe's arm tightened around him. He didn't respond.

The train jolted. Bodies shifted. Someone whimpered in the dark.

Jakob opened his eyes. He could barely make out shapes in the gloom. Just bodies. Huddled masses of despair.

A man's voice cried out. "Enough! I can't take it anymore. I can't."

No one said anything in response. People kept their heads down.

The man wouldn't stop. "We're all going to die. Don't you see? We're already dead."

Jakob had heard it before. From another. From the whispers.

The man's voice rose. Hysteria edged in. "They're going to kill us all. We should just end it now. End it before they can . . ."

"Stop it." The words were soft but firm. It came from the corner of the car.

Jakob turned his head. He squinted into the darkness. A figure moved. It was a man who had kept to himself since the beginning. Jakob didn't know his name.

The man stood. He was tall, even with the high ceiling of the railcar pressing down on him. He moved slowly, carefully, through the press of bodies.

"We are not dead," the man said. His voice was low and steady. "Not yet."

He reached the other man. Knelt beside him. "Brother, we must not give up."

The other man's laugh was bitter. "Give up? There's no hope in this hell?"

The tall man was quiet for a moment. Then he reached into his coat. He pulled out something small. A package wrapped in cloth.

"I have been saving this," he said. "For my children, if I found them. But perhaps . . . perhaps it can serve another purpose now."

He unwrapped the cloth. In the dim light, Jakob saw a small wooden toy train painted red. He offered it.

The other man's hand shook as he reached out.

"It reminds me of my children," the tall man said. "Do you have children?"

The other man nodded and wept.

"Take it," the tall man said. "So, you can hold on to them."

He took the toy train. He rubbed it and brought it into both hands, clasping it.

"Thank you," he said.

"If you will permit me," the tall man said. "I would like to offer a prayer."

Nobody spoke. But nobody objected.

The tall man began to pray. His voice was low and melodious. The words were in Hebrew. Jakob didn't understand them all, but he recognized the cadence. It was a prayer his father used to say.

As the man prayed, something changed in the car. The air seemed to lighten. The darkness didn't feel as oppressive.

Jakob felt Moshe stir beside him. The old man's voice joined the prayer. It was weak at first, then grew stronger.

Others joined in. Voices rose and fell. Some sang, others murmured. The prayer filled the car, pushing back the misery.

When it ended, there was silence. But it was a different kind of silence. Not the heavy silence of before, but a silence filled with something Jakob didn't understand.

The tall man spoke again. "We are still here," he said. "We are still alive. And as long as we live, we must not lose hope."

He looked around the car. In the dim light, Jakob could see tears on many faces.

"We do not know what lies ahead," the tall man continued. "But we are one people. One family."

The man holding the toy train spoke. "But how? How can we hope when we're headed for . . ."

He couldn't finish. They knew what was at the end.

The tall man was quiet for a moment. Then he said, "We hope because we must. We hope because we have to. If we don't, we've already lost before we get there."

He paused. "And we hope because we are Jews. Our people have faced darkness before. We have endured. We will endure again."

The railcar was silent. Jakob felt something stir inside him. A warmth. A tiny spark in the cold darkness.

Moshe's hand found his. The old man squeezed gently.

"What is your name?" Moshe asked the tall man.

"Names do not matter," he replied.

Moshe nodded. He understood. "Thank you," Moshe said. "For reminding us who we are."

The tall man nodded. He made his way back to his corner. The railcar settled into silence again.

But it was a different silence now. Jakob could feel it. The gloom had lifted, if only a little.

He leaned against Moshe and closed his eyes. For the first time in days, he didn't see darkness behind his eyelids. He saw his mother's smile. His father's strong hands. His sister's laughing face.

The train rolled on. It didn't stop. It kept moving through the night.

But inside the railcar, something had changed. There was a flame in his mind. Jakob held onto it. He nursed it, protected it. He knew it could go out at any moment. But for now, it burned.

And as long as it burned, they were alive. They were human. They were Jews.

The train rolled on. But they were no longer cargo, but people. Some with names, others without. But all with memories.

Jakob drifted off to sleep. His dreams were not of darkness but of light. Of home. Of family.

He woke to the sound of singing. Soft at first, then growing stronger. It was an old song, one his grandmother used to sing.

Others joined in. The song filled the car, pushing back the shadows.

Jakob sang too. His voice was weak, but it grew stronger with each word.

They sang of home. Of love. Of a future they might never see.

But they sang. And in singing, they lived.

The train rolled on. It didn't stop. But neither did they.

They were still here. Still alive. Still hoping.

And as long as they hoped, they were not defeated.

The song ended. The railcar fell silent again. But it was a silence full of life, of shared strength.

Jakob looked at Moshe. The old man's eyes were closed, but there was a small smile on his lips.

"Moshe," Jakob whispered.

"Yes, Jakob?"

"Thank you. For everything."

Moshe opened his eyes. He looked at Jakob. His hand found the Jakob's.

"No, Jakob," he said. "Thank you. For reminding an old man what's important in life."

The train rolled on. Into darkness. Into uncertainty.

They had found something in the darkness. Something that no one could take from them.

They had found each other. Found the strength to keep living, keep fighting, no matter what lay ahead.

The train rolled on. But they were ready. Ready to face whatever came next.

Together.

Arrival

The train stopped. The sudden silence was deafening. Jakob felt Moshe's hand tighten on his shoulder.

"Remember what I told you," Moshe said. His voice was low, urgent. "No matter what happens, you must survive."

Jakob nodded. He couldn't speak. Fear had stolen his voice.

The doors of the railcar slid open with a screech. A dim sunlight flooded in, blinding after days of darkness. Jakob blinked, his eyes watering.

Shouts filled the air. Harsh voices. German voices.

"Raus! Schnell!"

People began to move. A mass of bodies, pushing, shoving. Jakob felt himself being swept along.

"Stay close," Moshe said.

They stumbled out of the railcar. Jakob's legs trembled, ready to give out. He almost went down, but Moshe's hand held him steady. Jakob looked up. The sky was gray to him, flat.

The platform was chaos. Soldiers moved among the new arrivals. They carried clubs. Their eyes were dead.

Jakob looked around. He saw train tracks stretching away into the distance. He saw high fences topped with barbed wire. He saw watchtowers.

And beyond it all, he saw chimneys. Tall brick chimneys belching black smoke into the sky.

The smell hit him then. A smell like nothing he had ever known. Different than the smell of death he had known.

Jakob gagged. Moshe's hand tightened on his shoulder.

"Breathe through your mouth," Moshe said.

A whistle blew. Sharp and shrill.

"Men and boys to the right!" a voice shouted. "Women and children to the left!"

The crowd surged. Jakob felt himself being pulled away from Moshe.

"No!" he cried. He reached for the Moshe's hand.

Moshe's fingers brushed his. Then they were gone.

"Jakob!" Moshe's voice rose above the din. "Remember! Survive!"

Jakob tried to push back through the crowd. A gray uniform blocked his path.

"Move, boy," the man said. His voice was flat. Emotionless.

Jakob looked up. The man's eyes were as dead as his voice.

A shove from behind sent Jakob stumbling forward. He lost sight of Moshe in the crowd.

The line moved quickly. Too quickly. Jakob found himself facing a man in a different uniform. Black. The man's eyes flicked over him, cold and assessing.

"Right," the man said.

Another shove. Jakob was in a new line. All men and boys. No women. No children.

He looked back. He couldn't see Moshe anywhere.

The line shuffled forward. Jakob saw more men in black uniforms. They were separating people. Some went one way. Some went another.

An old man stumbled. A man in a gray uniform raised his club. The sound of the blow made Jakob flinch.

The line kept moving.

Jakob's turn came. A man in a black uniform looked at him. Jakob held his breath.

"Right," the man said.

Jakob hoped "right" was better than "left." But he wasn't sure.

He moved with the others. They were herded towards a gate. Above it, iron letters spelled out words Jakob didn't understand.

"Arbeit macht frei," a man next to him read. "Work makes you free."

The man laughed. It was a horrible sound.

Through the gate. Into the camp. The smell was stronger here. Jakob breathed through his mouth like Moshe had told him.

Moshe. Where was Moshe?

More shouting. More orders. Strip. Shower. Delousing.

Jakob did as he was told. His clothes were taken but he secretly kept the stone in his small hand. His head was shaved. He stood naked, shivering, as icy water sprayed over him.

New clothes. Striped uniform. Too big. Wooden shoes that didn't fit.

A number. Tattooed on his arm. It stung and made Jakob wince. Jakob stared at it. He wasn't Jakob anymore. He was a number.

More lines. More waiting. The sun was setting. Jakob's stomach growled. He couldn't remember the last time he had eaten.

Finally, they were led to barracks. Long wooden buildings. Bunks stacked three high.

"Find a spot," an older boy, a kapo barked.

Jakob climbed onto an empty bunk. The straw mattress was thin. He could feel the wooden slats beneath.

A bell rang. Lights out.

Jakob lay in the darkness. All around him, he could hear the sounds of the others breathing. Some were crying. Some were praying.

He thought of his family. His mother. His father. His little sister. Where were they? Were they alive?

He thought of Moshe. The old man's last words echoed in his head.

"Remember! Survive!"

Jakob closed his eyes. He squeezed the stone and made a promise to himself. To Moshe. To his family.

He would survive. No matter what.

The night passed. Jakob didn't sleep. He couldn't.

A whistle blew. Harsh and loud.

Jakob woke and looked around. Moshe was gone. The old man was a memory now. Jakob felt the emptiness beside him. It was a hollow feeling. Like hunger, but worse.

He sat up. No more crying. No more whispers. Just the sound of labored breathing as the others around him began to awaken.

Jakob remembered Moshe's words. "Hold onto hope," the Moshe had said. "It's all we have left."

Hope felt like a fragile thing now. As fragile as the first light of day seeping through the cracks in the railcar.

There was shouting outside and the doors swung open. More harsh voices. The sound of dogs barking.

"Out! Everyone out!" The voice was like a whip crack.

The boys sat on the ground. The wall was cold. The wind howled. It was cold enough that the air seemed to cut right through his clothes, thin as they were. The rations they had been given sat in their laps - some bread, a cup of water, and a thin soup that barely passed for food. He watched the others eat.

He didn't know their names.

Jakob took a sip of his soup then swallowed the last bite of bread. He tucked the stone into his fist. He carried it everywhere, always. He remembered his mother. His father. His sister. Moshe, his friend. He thought of them every day and every night.

"Eat slower," a boy told him. "You feel it more."

"I'm finished," Jakob said.

The boy nodded. There was nothing else to say.

They worked every day. Day after day after day. Digging. Lifting. Following orders. Staying alive. Jakob's body ached. He soon learned that if you got to know someone, they disappeared soon enough. Or worse. So they didn't play, didn't talk much, just moved through the days like shadows.

Boys shouldn't look like this, Jakob thought. Hollow-eyed. Skin pulled tight over bones. But there was no one left to care.

Work was the same every day. They dug, they lifted, they followed orders, and they stayed out of the guards' way. It was the only way to survive. Jakob had gotten used to the ache in his body, to the way his muscles felt like they were tearing themselves apart.

It was getting colder. One day, the cold settled deep into his bones, and something inside him changed. His head felt heavy, and every breath was a struggle. His legs shook when he walked. He tried to keep working, tried to hide the cough that wracked his chest, but it grew harder every day.

"You don't look well," a boy said.

"I'm fine," Jakob lied. He wasn't fine. He was sick, and he could feel it getting worse.

Days passed, maybe months or so. One morning, he couldn't get out of bed. His body refused to move, and his vision swam when he tried to sit up. He knew what this meant. He had seen it happen to others before. The ones who got sick didn't last long. The guards came for them.

The door to the barracks slammed open, and a soldier stepped inside. His boots crunched on the cold floorboards as he walked over to Jakob, who lay still, clutching the stone in his hand. The soldier looked down at him, his face hard and cold.

"You're no good anymore," he said. "Too sick to work."

Jakob stared up at him, not saying a word. He didn't have the strength to argue, didn't have the breath to speak. He just held the stone tighter, feeling the last warmth from his hand seep into the cold rock.

The soldier motioned. Another guard stepped forward. Jakob knew what would happen. He didn't fight. There was no point.

He thought of his family. And Moshe. He would hold on to them until the end.

Dawn

Jakob mustered what strength he had an stumbled to his feet. His legs were weak. He hadn't stood in days. He followed the guards and was pushed into a crowd, jostled by bodies moving towards a building.

Jakob squeezed the stone tightly.

There were men in black uniforms shouting orders. Dogs strained at their leashes, snarling and snapping.

Jakob looked for familiar faces. He saw only strangers. Lost and frightened, just like him.

A hand grabbed his arm. Rough. Uncaring. He was pushed along within the group. Some were crying. Others staggered silent, eyes wide with fear.

"Move!" The guard's voice was impatient. Angry.

They were herded like cattle. Away from the main barracks towards another building in the distance. It was a long walk. The ground was muddy. It sucked at Jakob's shoes.

Tall fences topped with barbed wire were on both sides of the path.

The stench of death hung in the air like a fog. Heavy. Suffocating.

Jakob thought of Moshe. Of the stories the old man had told. Of a world before all this. A world of warmth and laughter and family.

"Remember," Moshe had said." Never forget who you are. Where you come from. They can't take that from you."

Jakob held onto those words. They were a lifeline in a sea of despair.

The line of bodies moved slowly. Jakob could hear screams in the distance. The crack of gunfire. He tried not to listen. Tried not to think about what it meant.

A boy next to him stumbled. Fell to his knees in the mud. Jakob didn't have the strength to help him.

The boy looked up at Jakob. He didn't trust himself to speak.

They walked on. The building loomed closer. It was ugly. Utilitarian. A factory of death.

Jakob thought of his home. Of his mother's garden. The flowers she had tended with such care. How different it was from this place of mud and misery.

The line stopped. People bunched at the door. No one moved.

Jakob looked left. There, on the wire, sat a butterfly. Colorful wings against the gray, dull sky. It was still. Beautiful. More beautiful than anything. Jakob smiled. His hand reached out. He knew he couldn't touch it. But he wanted to. God, how he wanted to.

The line started to move again.

Jakob could see inside now. It was dark. Ominous.

He thought of running. Of breaking from the line and making a dash for the fence. Where would he go? And the guards. The dogs. But he didn't have the strength. He knew it was hopeless.

So he stood. And he waited. And he remembered.

He remembered his father's laugh. Deep and rich. The way it would fill a room.

He remembered his mother's hands. Soft and gentle. The way they would smooth his hair when he was upset.

He remembered his sister's smile. Bright and mischievous. The way it could light up her whole face.

And he remembered Moshe. The old man's wisdom. His kindness. The way he had become a father when Jakob needed one most.

He remembered something Moshe told him. Whispered in the dark of the railcar. "If we remember, we're free."

The line moved forward. Jakob was at the threshold now. He could feel the darkness reaching out for him. Hungry. Insatiable.

He took a deep breath. The air was foul. It clung to him, heavy and oppressive.

But underneath it, Jakob thought he could smell something else. Something faint and far away. The scent of his mother's garden. Of life and growth and hope.

It wasn't real. He knew that. But he held onto it anyway.

The guard at the door looked bored. Impatient. "Move," he barked.

Jakob stepped forward, following the others. Into the shadows. Into the unknown.

He squared his shoulders. He lifted his chin.

He couldn't see. Couldn't breathe. Panic clawed at his throat.

But then he remembered. Remembered who he was. Where he came from.

He took a step forward. Then another. And another. Along with the others. Crowded together.

He couldn't see where he was now. Didn't know what lay ahead. But he kept moving. One foot in front of the other.

Because that was what Moshe had taught him. To keep going. To never give up. To hold onto hope, even when all seemed lost.

The smell of death was overwhelming now. It filled his nostrils. Coated his tongue. But Jakob refused to let it defeat him.

He didn't know if he would survive this place. This factory of death. But he wasn't afraid. Because that was what Moshe had taught him. What his parents had taught him. What life had taught him.

He heard the door shut. It was a dull thud. A final, undeniable seal. The darkness was complete now. Absolute. It engulfed him, complete and utter. He was into the unknown, carrying with him the light of memory.

He shut his eyes tight. The stone was cold in his hand. He squeezed it hard. His breath came slow and deep. There was a metallic tang on his tongue.

Cold and empty seconds. That's all he felt. Then there was nothing at all.

Outside, the butterfly on the barbed wire fluttered its wings. Once. Twice. Then it was gone. Free.

ABOUT THE AUTHOR

Philip Mazza is a novelist with a boundless imagination, captivating readers with the epic fantasy series *The Harrow Saga*. Born in New York in 1959, he earned a degree in Business from LeMoyne College and an MBA, later holding leadership roles in human resources and operations. Now a professor at the Madden School of Business and Economics, Philip dedicates his time to his students and writing. *Beneath the Ashen Sky* is his eighth literary work. He and his wife enjoy travel and continue to live in upstate New York.

www.ingramcontent.com/pod-product-compliance
Lightning Source LLC
Chambersburg PA
CBHW032111170626
46808CB00008B/3015